Mystery of the Old Mill

By
Laura E. Federmeyer

All characters are fictional. The Addison Blockhouse and the Old Sugar Mill are real. The Blockhouse is on Florida State property. Years ago, the Park Service used to have canoe trips to the old dock for tourists to walk in to see the Blockhouse. Now, the dock is in unsafe condition and no plans to restore it.

The Old Sugar Mill (McCrae) is on private property and not accessible

See added sheet from Florida Division of Recreation & Parks for added info on both properties.

THIS BOOK IS DEDICATED TO:

My friend, Hazel Sweat (now deceased) who madc it possible for me to Ride the woods on my horse and discover the Blockhouse and The Old Mill.

MYSTERY OF THE OLD MILL

By

Laura E. Federmeyer

Chapter One

Charlie jabbed the heels of her soiled sneakers into her fat cream colored pony's sides. Quickly the pony drove its strong legs faster along the hard packed dirt trail. With her long blonde hair streaming out behind her, Charlie leaned over the pony's neck. Long shadows across the trail told her she was going to be late. The eight year old lifted her head to let the wind whip across her face. Her cheeks dimpled in pleasure at the feel of speed. Oh how she loved a running horse!

A wider trail branched off to the right that led out of the woods and the road toward home. Peanut needed no further urging to veer to the right and run for home.

Charlie didn't see the camouflaged marked jeep sitting deep in the bushes on the other trail. She was more focused on getting out of the woods and home. Rules had been broken. She was not supposed to ride alone in the woods.

A grey bearded man jerked his head up at the sudden sound of horse's hooves on the trail. The surprise of someone's presence almost caused him to drop his cigarette in his lap. With a scowl on his face, he watched the young rider fly by.

Where had she been? Did she find the Mill? Waiting until he felt safe and didn't hear the rider's horse, he started the jeep's engine. Shifting the gears, he drove back down the trail Charlie had just left.

Charlie slowed Peanut down as they neared the barn. Throwing a leg over the pony's neck, she dropped to the ground when Peanut came to a stop. Quickly she removed the saddle pad and led the pony into the barn where she put it into its stall.

While she was putting her pad and bridle in the tack room, she heard her brother David whistling. She had hoped to get her chores done without getting caught.

David, a tall lanky fifteen year old glanced over and saw the pony now in its stall. Sweat marks on its back showed the outline of where the saddle pad had been.

"Charlie, Are you still in here?"

She poked her head around the corner of the feed room. "Need any help?" she called, ignoring his question. Wrinkling up her nose, she tried to look innocent.

Ignoring her question, David eyed her with his piercing blue eyes. Frowning, he asked. "Where were you?"

"Just riding."

"Who with?"

"Peanut, of course." She paused. "No one." She mumbled loud enough for her ears only.

"I can't hear you." replied David in a sing-song voice. His hands were on the hips of his faded jeans and his manner demanded a straight answer.

Charlie nibbled on her lower lip and stole a glance up at him.

"No one, okay? Nothing happened. I'm fine." She shot back, feeling a little guilty. This was her first time getting caught riding alone.

"Okay, okay, don't get huffy. Here. Feed the horses." He shoved a full bucket of feed into her hands. With his other hand, he ruffled her hair. "You'd better not do it again, kid."

"I'll try to remember."

Charlie hefted the heavy bucket over to the grey mare and dumped half into her feed bucket. She then took the rest over to Peanut. Listening to them munch on their grain got her to wonder what they were having for dinner.

She refilled the bucket and fed the other two horses in the barn that belonged to their parents. David came along the hallway with his arms loaded with hay for the horses.

"Listen, Charlie, I won't tell mom or dad this time, but try to be more careful. Maybe we can call Todd and Lisa and we can all go riding Saturday. Mom might fix us a picnic lunch.."

"That sounds great. Thanks. I hear dad's car."

A dark blue van pulled into the driveway stopping in the carport. A tall lean sandy-haired man stepped out. His suit coat was slung over his shoulder and his tie was already loose around his neck, the shirt's top button undone. A briefcase swung alongside his left leg as he walked toward the house. Stopping, he waited for David and Charlie to come up from the barn so they could walk into the house together.

"Hi, Dad. The chores are all done. Have a good day?"

"It's always better when I get home. Everyone wanted to be taken care of at once. Sherry, my new secretary, decided to take the day off and left a girl who never worked front desk in charge. There are probably missing files everywhere. It was a rat race today. Glad to be home. What's for dinner?"

"We don't know, but it is starting to smell good."

Inside the kitchen, the smell of a beef stew assailed their noses. Everyone breathed in the wonderful aroma as they peeked in at the Mom. She turned toward them offering them a warm smile and greeting before turning back to the bubbling stew. Everyone had to shower and change before dinner would be served.

Charlie hopped on one foot as she tried to pull on a clean pair of sneakers. She heard

David already going down the stairs.

Grabbing a pony tail twist off her dresser, she ducked her head down and grabbed a handful of her hair, wrapping the twist around the bunch. Swinging it loose, she took one glance in the mirror before leaving her room.

The dining room table was already set and everyone was seated when Charlie came up to the table. David said the blessing and his Dad read a scripture from his Bible. The usual table conversation followed and David asked their Mom, Jean, if she could pack a lunch for their ride Saturday morning.

"It will be a good day according to the weatherman. Are you going to invite Todd and Lisa or go alone?"

"We are going to call after we eat."

Todd and Lisa told them they could go. Their Mom had just made brownies and chocolate chip cookies. They would bring them for their dessert. Charlie was elated.

Rarely did her brother offer to ride with her, let alone spend the whole day with her. Todd would keep him entertained while her and Lisa talked and enjoyed the ride. She could show them some new trails the developers had opened up while developing a nearby property. She had been down several of them and they all seemed to lead into some interesting spots along the river or deeper into the woods.

Charlie wasn't too sure about how much she should let on that she knew about the new trails, though. David would really have a fit about her going alone then. She chewed on her pencil as she looked down at her homework on the desk. The answers to the questions soon came to her and she began to write.

There was also an essay that needed to be started soon. A science project was due sometime next month. Music broke the silence of her thoughts. David was playing his music a little too loud.

Her cheeks dimpled. Mom would be calling up the stairs in a few minutes to tell him to quiet down. Just above a whisper, she began counting. She only reached ten before Mom's voice came up the stairs.

Charlie laughed. The humdrum of studying was broken by the music incident. Her thoughts drifted on toward the Saturday ride. She lived to ride and couldn't wait.

Saturday morning turned out to be a beautiful day. Clear blue skies with a gentle breeze blowing small fluffy white clouds overhead made the day perfect. Several mockingbirds chirped from a nearby tree. A lone hawk winged across the sky floating on the air currents.

Charlie watched the hawk as she tightened the red bareback pad onto Peanut's back. Peanut's golden coat shone brightly in the sunshine. His creamy white mane and tail were free of tangles. She could hardly wait to get going.

Glancing over at the hitching post, she watched David put the bridle on his grey mare. She also shone from a good brushing. The grey's ears flipped forward as her head came up looking toward the driveway. Peanut's head also turned as he nickered a greeting as two riders came up the driveway.

A slim tanned arm was raised in greeting. Lisa waved to Charlie as she reined her black and white paint pony toward them. Her long silky black hair was braided in one large braid down her back. Nine year old Lisa put her weight on her left foot and swung down from her saddle. Dropping the reins of her pony, she came over to Charlie.

Charlie slowly shook her head, amazed that Lisa's pony would stay in the same spot. It had been trained to ground tie.

"Lisa, you've got to show me how you get your pony to do that."

Lisa laughed. "If you can keep Peanut from eating everything around him, it would be easy."

"What's with Todd? He don't look too happy to be here."

Both girls looked over at the boy sitting on the brown gelding. Todd was acting as if he really didn't want to be there. Todd loved his horse, but right now video games with his Nintendo DS held his interest. He was voicing his thoughts to David, who was listening. He liked video games, too, but would rather be outdoors, even though it meant 'babysitting' his sister.

"Just don't take it as a 'babysitting' day. Charlie says there are new trails we can go on to explore. My Mom packed us a picnic lunch. Your Mom made brownies and chocolate chip cookies, my favorites. We will have a great time." said David.

Todd brightened up at the thought of eating someone else's food. His Mom made great desserts, but was not so great a cook otherwise.

Hearing the screen door slam, Todd looked over toward the house as David's Mom came out carrying saddlebags stuffed with food. Lisa met her halfway to add the bags of cookies and brownies to the saddlebags.

"Do you know what time you all will be getting back? I don't want to send out a search party."

David looked at his watch. It was nine o'clock.

"Maybe two or three, Mom. I need to do some studying before chores tonight."

"All right. Have fun and be careful. I won't worry about you getting lost because the horses know the way home."

David tied the heavy saddlebags behind his saddle and turned his mare around to mount. Lisa got back on her pony and Charlie vaulted onto Peanut's back.

"Bye, Mom." replied Charlie as she gathered up the reins to turn Peanut around toward the woods. Todd took all four lead ropes and halters fastening them to the back of his saddle. They would have them to tie out the horses while they ate lunch.

David let Lisa and Charlie go first since they seemed to know where they were going. He talked to Todd first about school, their science project, then drifted over to their latest Nintendo game.

Squirrels chattered in the trees, Mockingbirds sang to the kids as they rode along at a slow ambling pace. Several Banana Spiders were in their webs across parts of the trail that had to be ducked, to leave the spider alone.

Lisa pulled her Miami Dolphin hat down tighter on her head. Her braided pony tail kept it loose. Taking the hat off, she undid the sizing strap and stuck her tail through the opening, then fixed the strap. Now, the ponytail would not bother her again with the hat securely on her head.

She turned her attention toward looking for wildlife. Riding with Charlie was a treat that she didn't get very often. Other things kept her busy and she was not allowed to ride out of her yard alone, either. Charlie was lucky to have all these woods to ride in whenever she took the notion.

Snatches of the boy's conversation reached hear ears. Nintendo! They were talking about their stupid video games! Here they were in the great outdoors on a perfect sunny day and they were talking about stuff that would keep them inside. She reached over and patted her pony's neck.

On the ground under them, were old deer tracks. Her thoughts drifted to maybe seeing deer while they were out on their 'adventure' today.

Charlie took a trail off to the right that was only wide enough for riding single file. She hadn't been down this particular trail and was curious as to where it went. She rode slowly so she could brush back the palmetto fans and duck under the spider webs. Lisa made a little squeal as she got too close to a spider web. Charlie chuckled to herself. Lisa was so … She couldn't think of a word for it. Lisa stayed indoors too much. Maybe she could come and ride with her so David would leave her alone. As the single trail widened and split in a fork, Charlie stopped. David and Todd caught up and David decided to lead.

Chapter Two

David addressed the other riders.

"Here's a trail that looks wide enough to ride through. Want to see where it goes? Or do you want to stay on the wide trail?"

"We could try it. There are others further along that are wider and better to travel. Let's be adventurous and try this one for a short while."

"Okay, let me lead, then." replied David.

Everyone nodded in agreement. David led them though the narrow opening between the brush. Large clumps of palmettos had to be circled to follow the faint trail. As they came around a large stand of palmettos, a small clearing opened out before them.

In the middle of it stood partial walls of grey tabby stone of some kind of building. Green vines covered the stone walls of what was once a productive sugar mill.

"Wow! What is that?" exclaimed Todd. They had not lived in Florida very long and had never seen any historical sugar cane mills.

"It looks like an old sugar mill ruins. See? There's a big iron vat over there. Be careful for there could be an uncovered well near-by."

"Let's get down and explore."

Todd handed out the lead ropes with their horse's halters attached. Everyone tied their horses to a nearby tree before they began to slowly search the area.

David was unsure about the area. Something was sort of strange about the place.

Rough grey stone called Tabby was covered with different kinds of vines. Seashells in the rocks drew Lisa's attention. She loved to collect different kinds when they visited the beach.

Todd went to the old rusty machinery that stood beside the crumbling walls. David stayed back as sort of a guard. He didn't want to poke around. As he walked around, he did a double take at some faint tire tracks.

Slowly he scraped his foot across the leaves covering the tracks. Before he knew it, he had cleared a well worn trail off toward the main trail leading into the woods. Someone was coming here fairly regular.

They had better leave. There had not been any 'Do Not Trespass' signs. He was curious. Why would anyone be coming here? Nothing seemed out of place or disturbed, but they had taken great care to cover their tracks.

Looking up, David saw the others seemed to be getting the horses ready to remount. Quickly he scuffed back the leaves over the trail he had uncovered. He moved over to his horse. Checking the saddle cinch to make sure it was tight, he prepared to mount.

He took off the halter and handed it back to Todd to tie with the others on the back of his saddle. Easily, then, he swung into the saddle reining the mare around and back to the trail. His blue eyes swept over the area to make sure they didn't leave any traces of their being there. Charlie moved up with her pony to take over the lead. David shook his head.

"Let me keep leading until we get to the main trail. It should be off this way."

He kneed the mare and started off. "We'll go to the river and have lunch. I'm getting a little saddle sore."

The others chuckled. So were they, but they wouldn't admit it. David kept the horses off the main trail hoping to hide their tracks if the people coming there would see them. No one else made any comment about staying off the faint trail. David tried to look for landmarks when they came out on the main trail in case he wanted to return to the Mill. It could be that some of the land developers were coming there to survey. Whatever it was, he was getting curious. He knew that Charlie would too, if she had seen the tracks.

As the trail widened, Todd came up beside David and Lisa passed them with Charlie, as they took the lead to the River. David fought his inner thoughts as he tried to focus on Todd and what he had to say. The longer Todd talked, the further from his mind went the Mill. His horse stretched out her neck to grab some tall grass on the side of the trail. The reins slipped through his fingers forcing his full attention on his horse.

As they came out onto the main trail, off to the left behind a huge Magnolia tree stood the remains of Addison's Blockhouse. It was built in the early 1800's and manned by soldiers to fight the Seminole Indians when they were at war. The kids had been there several times and couldn't see how all the men could move about in the small space available and still be able to fight.

David knew that the Florida Park Service used to bring guests from the campground in canoes to visit the Blockhouse. Now, the wooden dock was in bad shape and not safe. They had visited the Blockhouse several times when they had ridden to the river. This time they passed the trail to the Blockhouse and rode on toward the river.

Tall grass beckoned to all four horses as they were fastened on long lead ropes. Hungrily they all chomped away once they were free of their riders, as if it was the last grass ever to reach their mouths. Through some palm trees and brush, the river could be seen.

An old wooden dock stood alongside the

shore with only a few boards left fastened to the posts that held it to the shoreline. David set the saddlebags down on a large tree stump.

Charlie opened the bags, reaching inside for the sandwiches. She handed everyone a sandwich and bag of chips. Lisa opened the bag of homemade cookies. Todd brought the thermos of cold drink and cups. David had the paper plates.

Several spots along the bank showed signs that something had been sitting there. Large squares, probably boxes were outlined by the yellowed grass near the bank. David frowned. The others hadn't noticed the marks on the grass as yet. It wouldn't be long before they started looking around.

Now he wondered if the dock had been used. Taking his sandwich, David walked over to the rundown dock. It still looked unsafe and there were no level boards to step out of a boat onto.

Along the edge of the bank, though, the grass was trampled down. Someone was coming there and frequently. Excitement flowed through him with a cold chill running down his spine.

Something mysterious and probably crooked was taking place. In their own back yard, almost! He would have to try to convince Charlie not to ride alone or stay out of this area. It would be like trying to catch a greased pig. Charlie would not pay attention or take orders.

Charlie slowly chewed her third cookie. She looked around to see where David had gone. As her gaze took in the surrounding area, she saw the yellowed grass in the square shapes. Something had been sitting there! Should she mention it to the others? Just as she opened her mouth, David returned.

"Everyone ready to go?" asked David as he walked up beside Charlie. He put a hand on her shoulder. He could tell she had seen the yellowed grass and was ready to say something to the others.

"But….I wanted to tell everyone about….."

David put a finger to his lips barely talking out loud. "No. Let's keep it quiet. You and me will talk later. We might be trespassing. Come on. Make sure all of you clean up your mess and put it back in the saddlebags."

Charlie looked up at her brother with new respect. He was actually going to share something he saw with her.

All the way back towards home, Charlie was beside herself. All kinds of sinister imagination ideas were running through her mind. What kind of strange activity was going on back here along the river? Her mind raced with all the possibilities. She imagined herself as a heroine who single-handily brought the criminals to justice. Were they drug dealers, smugglers or criminals just looking for a place to hide from the authorities? The local papers and National ones would carry the story and her picture would be on their front pages.

Lisa tapped her on the arm as she rode up beside her. "Charlie, where does this trail go?"

Charlie jumped out of her dream and back to the present. A path was leading off to the right coming back from the river. "That one goes to the old Addison Blockhouse. See the big Magnolia Tree? That is where to turn toward the Blockhouse. We've been there before. We could see it again if you want. I think there is another trail heading home on the other side."

Both girls looked back for a 'go ahead' sign from the boys. They agreed with a nod of their heads. When they reached the large Magnolia tree, they turned toward the right onto the trail to the Blockhouse. Several old aluminum beer cans were scattered about. An old deer stand was propped up against a tree. No one had been there since fall hunting season. Inwardly David sighed in relief. So far no one knew of their presence.

He had to get the group farther from the main road.

Suddenly David's mare flipped her ears forward and came to an abrupt halt. Her nostrils flared as her body started to tremble.

"Deer." replied David quietly. "She always does this when there are some around."

The others watched and soon two small brown deer moved across the open area several feet from where they stood, still partially hidden by the palmettos. It was their first time seeing deer this far back in the woods. All four held their breath, hoping the deer would stay and not run. The larger one flipped its black tipped ears. She stood motionless as if listening to the forest sounds.

Time seemed to stand still as the kids watched; fascinated by the beauty of the deer. Slowly the deer moved across the open area and disappeared in the palmetto scrub. No one talked for several minutes as they too moved in the opposite direction.

A half hour later the riders circled the lake near home. Through a narrow trail between the two lakes, they rode single file. Branches from the brush and trees along the path had to be ducked to avoid the thorns on the flowering brush. All four of them bent low over their horse's neck to avoid the low branches. Lisa used one hand to hold onto her hat.

"Watch out for that vine on the right. It has thorns."

Respectively everyone avoided the vine. Reaching the halfway point, a narrow swift moving stream of water flowed between the two lakes.

Here, they let the horses take their turns

drinking the fresh water. David took his feet out of his stirrups. His legs were beginning to ache. Was he ever going to be sore tomorrow!

Todd called out to him. "Look, David. There's an Osprey on that old dead tree."

David followed Todd's arm as he pointed to a dead tree up on the trail above the lakes. Like a large hand stretching toward the sky the dead tree towered above the young green cedar trees. On one of its branches sat a young Osprey. As the riders came up the small sandy hill and onto the road that wound past the tree, the Osprey took flight. It's wings were extended all the way out to catch the air currants.

"Gosh, he's beautiful! Look how it catches the breezes to move about. I sure wouldn't mind flying like that for an hour or so." replied Todd, dreamily. His passion was flying. He was counting the days and years when he would be tall and heavy enough to hang glide. Sitting on his horse, Todd watched the Osprey swing over the lake, then dive straight down, skimming the surface. Seconds later, a small fish was squirming in its strong talons as the Osprey once more took flight toward a nearby Oak tree. Lost in its leaf covered branches, it landed to eat its meal.

"Wonder what Mom is having for dinner." said Charlie as she stretched upright on Peanut's back. Even she was feeling stiff from riding all day. Late afternoon shadows followed the four along the last mile of their ride for home.

Mrs. Thomas looked out the bay window near her kitchen sink. Smiling, she turned toward the refrigerator for the cold drinks.

Her horse riders had returned safely. By the way they were sitting in their saddles, they were sore and tired. The kitchen clock showed three o'clock. They had been gone six hours. By the time they finished with the horses, she would have time to get the last of the cookies out of the oven.

A peanut butter aroma floated through the kitchen. Her oatmeal ones were already done and in their cookie jar. Footsteps on the porch caused her to turn expectantly toward the door. Lisa and Todd walked in followed by Charlie.

"Hello, Mrs. Thomas."

"Hi, Todd, Lisa. How was the day, Charlie?"

"We had a great time." Sniffing the air, "Mmmm. Peanut Butter cookies. We'll get our hands washed. David will be in soon. He went to turn the horses into the corral so they could roll."

"All four of them?"

"Yeah. We'll saddle back up later. David said he has a new Nintendo game to show me."

"I believe it is a good one and hard to finish. I have trouble getting him back onto his homework. I have cold drinks and cookies for all of you."

"Thanks. I might like to eat mine standing up."

Lisa looked over at Charlie and winked. "Men. They just can't take it."

Charlie grinned and reached for another cookie. She was feeling stiff and sore too, but would not admit it.

After Todd and Lisa left, Charlie followed David out to the barn to take care of the horses. David sat down on a bale of hay. Somehow he had to explain today's events to Charlie. Would she listen? Charlie sat down on another bale and looked at him.

"Well? What did you make of those yellowed grass marks along the river?"

David, for a second, almost was not going to tell her anything, but that would only make her curious and cause her to maybe get into trouble.

"They looked like boxes of something had been sitting there for some time. The dock had been used, but I don't see how. There's not a flat board on the whole structure."

"Should we tell anyone? Maybe the police?"

"Not yet. We are not sure what is going on and if that property is privately owned. We might get in trouble for trespassing. Listen, I know you are going to get too curious, but there is or was something going on at that old Mill also. I uncovered some tire tracks at the Mill leading to the main road and heading for the river. We need to be careful when we ride in the woods from now on and stay back out of that area. Can I count on your cooperation?"

Charlie held one hand behind her back with her fingers crossed. She tried to look David in the eye. She would have to venture back there again someday soon to see if she could find out anything.

With school and homework, it would have to be on the weekend. Hopefully David might be talked into riding with her or be busy trying to master his video game.

They finished up at the barn with the horses freshly brushed and put into their stalls for their meal. Charlie stretched her aching arm muscles. David watched and grinned. He was sore, too, but wouldn't let on. At least not to a little sister!

Charlie sat in her room flipping through a magazine listening to David's video game music. He was trying so hard to get to a different level of the game! He should be working on his science project just like she should be doing. Several books lay open on her desk showing drawings of what she wanted to do for hers.

Reluctantly she got off the bed, tossing the

magazine aside. As she approached the desk, she thought of what she would write about! Now she scrambled to grab a pen and paper from her top desk drawer and sit down at the same time.

Shoving back a couple of the open books, she made room on the desktop to write. With head bent and her pen quickly moving over the paper, she was now engrossed in her work.

A half smile jerked up her lips. The dimple in her cheek showed as she set that paper aside and stretched out an empty one to continue. One of the books was pulled over in front of her as she scanned the pages. Holding one finger on a spot in the book, she copied down the words.

Chapter Three

Back off the trail well hidden among the palmetto scrub sat a camouflaged jeep. Grey sideburns stood out on his evenly tanned face. A bearded stubble showed grey hairs among the hairs growing on his chin. An unlit cigarette hung from the corner of his mouth.

Anger flashed in his brown eyes as he watched the kids pass by. Where had they been? Hopefully they had not been near the river and the old dock. This was the second time in two weeks that he had seen horseback riders on this main trail to the river.

After what he considered a safe time, Ralph turned the key in the jeep's ignition. As the engine came to life, he shifted gears. Driving down the main road, he headed toward the river dock.

At the place where David led them out of the woods from the Mill, Ralph saw a track. Swearing half aloud, he braked the jeep. Leaving the engine running, he climbed out to look at the tracks.

He crouched down to look closer, but couldn't tell whether they had come from that way or just happened to step off the grass where the track could be made. Checking the other side of the road was empty of tracks. None were back the way he had come. They were coming from the river.

Ralph climbed back into the jeep and drove on toward the river and braked the jeep. The boat would be coming along shortly. Thankfully the kids had left the area and missed hearing the boat coming toward the old dock.

As he walked toward the dock, he spotted where the kids had sat to eat their lunch and had tied their horses. He was glad they hadn't come earlier. Looking around, he also noted that the kids had picked up all their trash and left no signs of them being there at all.

In the distance, he heard the steady hum of a boat motor. Ralph stayed back out of sight, but in a position where he could see the boat coming. The motor sounded louder as a small blue and white boat came slowly around the bend.

One man was at the wheel. The direction of the boat was heading for the old dock. Ralph stepped out from behind the tree; his hand loosely holding the walnut grip of his .38 revolver.

The younger man in the boat, waved to Ralph as he cut the engine and tossed Ralph the rope. Ralph grabbed the rope and tied it to a nearby tree, then pulled the boat closer so Gary could step out.

Gary cut the motor completely and hopped onto the bank. He shoved his dirty blonde hair back under the black ball cap and replaced the cap. He grinned at Ralph.

"Hello, Ralph."

"Did you bring the stuff?" asked Ralph as he lit the cigarette.

"Sure. Are you going to take it to the Mill?"

"I am. Some kids on horseback was just here. I'm not sure if they found the Old Mill or not."

"Have you found their tracks around the Mill?"

Ralph shook his head. "I haven't had time to check. Let's get you unloaded."

Three large boxes were unloaded and placed on the grass over the yellowed grass. Gary helped Ralph load the boxes into the back of the jeep. He then climbed back into the boat and Ralph untied the rope. The motor came to life and Gary waved so long to Ralph.

Quickly he guided the boat around and sped off the way he had come. Ralph walked to his jeep and began covering up the boxes. He would just open a box and take out part to carry with him to town. Some of the locals were waiting for this shipment and had their money ready to buy all that Ralph would give them.

Ralph checked around the Mill for possible signs of the kids and their horses being there. He didn't find any traces so he went directly to the well where he was storing the boxes.

Carefully he swept leaves back off the lid of the well. He then lowered each box down into the dark well. Ralph then replaced the lid and spread more leaves over the top and made an extra effort to cover his own tire tracks.

Somehow he would have to come up with a way to scare the kids enough to keep them out of the area. Maybe the ruins could be haunted with Seminole Indians. Grinning, he turned onto the paved road. He had a perfect plan. All he needed would be the costume and some props.

* * *

Sunday after Church and dinner, David went to his room. He changed into his everyday clothes and picked up his camera. As he walked past Charlie's room, he stuck his head in on his way downstairs.

"Want to go for a quick ride?"

Charlie glanced up from tying her tennis shoes. Seeing the camera in his hand, she nodded. They were going back to the Mill!

"We'll take some pictures and come back. I don't want to stay very long."

"If you can keep your mare from eating all the grass from here to there it will be a quick ride."

David ruffled her hair and laughed. "Sure. Be sure to wear your watch."

With the horses ready, they mounted and took off at a slow lope. Quickly they covered the ground to the main trail into the woods. Slowing, they single filed down the trail with David leading. Suddenly David reined in the mare. Charlie pulled back on her reins bringing Peanut up alongside him.

"What?…" started Charlie.

David pointed to the jeep tracks on the main road. "Do you suppose they saw us?"

"It's possible. They could be the security for the property. Come on. Let's get going."

Nudging the horses, they once more continued at a walk. Both kept their eyes and ears open for any sign of the vehicle.

Coming to the trail that cut off to the Mill, they saw the double tracks coming from the Mill and going there. Other tracks showed heading toward the river and back. Ralph had thought he had covered his tracks, but the wind had blown most of the leaf covering away.

"Something is definitely going on here. Let's get our pictures and leave the back way. Keep on the grass here so our tracks will not show very much."

They couldn't see where anything had been

disturbed, but David didn't want to stick around to look. He took almost a full roll of film from every angle. Charlie stayed on her horse and waited. David mounted the mare and they left by the way they had originally found the Mill.

School and bad weather combined kept the kids out of the woods and indoors. David's pictures had all come out. Tentatively he showed them to several teachers. The Mill had been a large working sugar cane grinding and syrup making plantation. During the Seminole Indian raids along the river in 1836, it had been burned down. The plantation owners being burned out, never rebuilt. No one seemed to know who owned the property now.

With the weather cleared and the rain soaked ground drying up, the riders began to venture into the woods once more. David and Charlie made several rides in the general area to search out new trails that would quicken their trips to and fro.

They found a new trail to come in by the Addison Blockhouse. This way, they could go directly to the river without being on the main trail for the man in the jeep to see them. Both were dying of curiosity. Even today, it was late in the afternoon and it was to be a short ride. Several days of rain had made most of the trails impassable.

They had just reached the Magnolia tree when sounds of a jeep reached them. Quickly they reined their horses around and got far off the trail and out of sight.

On the way to the river Ralph drove past the Magnolia tree. David and Charlie saw him for the first time. They watched him drive on toward the river unmindful of someone watching him from the woods. Letting plenty of time to elapse, they moved the horses back to the main trail.

"We'll follow him and see what he is doing. Maybe we can get close enough to hear what they say if he meets someone at the river."

"We didn't bring any tie ropes for the horses. Your mare will not stay in one spot."

"Right. We'll ride close enough and then you can stay with the horses. I know you want to go, too, but I can run faster. I'll need to know you're here with the horses."

Reluctantly Charlie agreed. She would worry about them, too, if they both walked off and left them for any length of time. Peanut had been trained to stay tied, but Liz was a eater and would be trying to get loose to eat what she couldn't reach. If this was going to be dangerous, they needed a reliable get-a-way.

Finding a wide spot off the road and hidden, they dismounted.

"Listen." said Charlie. "I hear a boat motor."

"Yeah. I'd better get going. Next time we will bring the ropes." He touched her shoulder, then trotted off through the brush.

With a small grin on her face, Charlie watched him go. Was he ever going to be covered with ticks! David's horse, Liz, spotted a clump of grass and started to reach for it. Charlie turned her attention to the big mare. She had her hands full now.

Ralph was standing at the dock smoking a cigarette when David crouched nearby downwind. He heard the boat motor getting louder and soon it came to the dock. The man they had followed in the jeep was tying the boat to a tree and holding it steady for the younger man to come ashore.

"Howdy, Ralph. How's business?"

"Great. I'm almost out. Did you get a full load?"

"No. I only was able to get half of it. Someone down the line is suspicious so they are laying low. They suggested we do the same."

"Why? I haven't seen those kid's horse tracks for several weeks. They must have decided to ride elsewhere or are too busy. The authorities have not been asking questions at the bar, so I doubt if they even reported anything suspicious going on out here."

Gary started handing Ralph the first box. Ralph carried it over and set it down on the ground, returning for the second box. What he had so far would not last very long at all. He had some new customers and several of the older ones were now hooked on the drugs. Gary handed Ralph the last box and walked over and sat down on one of them.

"Do you happen to have a cold one? It gets hot out there on the river."

"Sure."

David had heard enough. He focused his camera and took their pictures. He made several shots to make sure at least one of them came out. Slowly he eased back from his crouched position. Carefully he picked his way through the palmettos to where Charlie waited with the horses.

She almost screamed when he came up so quietly. She breathed a big sigh of relief. She stood up, stretching aching leg muscles from crouching so long while she waited for David to return.

"What did you find out?"

"They know about us, but not who we are. I'm glad we didn't report it to the authorities; otherwise they would be stopping their operations. They have seen our tracks and the fact that it has been raining and washed out the trails, they are not suspicious any longer. We're going to have to quit riding back here for awhile. Let's stay here and see if he drives out and back toward town or over to the Mill. We'll then go back home after he leaves the area. There was a guy in a boat. He didn't look familiar. The man in the jeep is named Ralph. Shush..... Here comes the jeep."

Sure enough the jeep sped on by heading straight on out toward the main road and town. Ralph was taking the whole shipment with him. He didn't have to worry about the swarming mosquitoes that were surely at the Mill site.

On the ride home, David described both men so Charlie would recognize either of them if they saw them in town. Both were thoughtful knowing now one of the mysteries was solved. Some of their school friends could be victims of this dangerous cargo.

Drugs were everywhere in all classes of people. It was hard to say 'no' and survive the peer pressure.

Todd grabbed the notebook from his school locker, jamming his history book in the notebook's place. One of these days he needed to take time to clean out his locker. Today was not it.

He held back the books and paper that threatened to fall out on the floor, then slammed the door shut snapping the combination lock in place. As he turned around to head for his next class, he saw David coming toward him. He lifted a hand in greeting.

"David, I've got something I want to show you after school. Meet me out by the picnic table."

"Okay. Want to go riding with the girls Saturday?"

"Sounds okay by me if we can play your

Nintendo game later."

"Sure. See ya."

David ran a hand through his hair as he waited for Todd to reach the picnic table where he waited. Todd opened the envelope upon reaching David.

"I saw a man in a jeep the other day in town and took his picture. Is he the same man you saw in the woods?"

David looked at the photograph. There was the man called Ralph behind the wheel of a jeep.

"Yes, that's him. We have to find out who he is. We know is name is Ralph."

"He hangs out at Scooters playing pool."

"You have to be eighteen to get in there to play pool. We can't find out anything from across the street or looking in the window."

"Who do we know that would do something for us?"

"How about Roger? He's a fair pool player and he probably knows some of the guys who hang out there."

"Where does Roger work?"

"Mac's Garage. Come on."

Chapter Four

David and Todd walked to the parking lot where David's moped was parked. They climbed on and rode to Mac's Garage. Blonde headed Roger was just sliding out from under a car when the boys drove up into the parking lot.

Todd saw him sliding out, recognizing him as his friend Roger. Roger stood up, wiping his greasy hands on his coveralls. Greasy smudges on his cheeks made him look unshaven. His hair was ruffled and in need of a haircut.

"Hi, fellows. What brings you here?"

"We wanted to talk to you. Have you got a few minutes?"

"Sure. Want a cold drink? I'm taking a break."

"I'll buy." replied David as he began digging coins from his pocket.

With drinks in hand, they all sat down on the warped picnic table in the shade of the building. Todd showed him the picture of Ralph in the jeep.

"This is the man we need to find out about. He hangs around Scooters. We think he and several others are up to something in the woods near our place and we're sure it is illegal. We were wondering if you could just hang out at Scooters a couple of nights and see if he is there and maybe listen in on his conversations."

"That's Ralph Snyder. He runs the lawn mower shop on Jefferson. I really don't know anything about him other than he likes to play pool at Scooters and drive his jeep. How soon do you need to know?"

"As soon as possible. We don't know what he is hiding at the Mill. Someone is bringing it in by boat. He brings it to town and distributes it here. We were hoping you could play a couple games of pool and just listen."

Roger looked at the two boys. He knew the boys were straight and meant well. Maybe there was something going on in their little town. He had heard talk about drugs coming in, but no one knew where or how. He crushed his soda can and tossed it into the trash barrel. It sounded like they had a mystery to solve and he could become an important part of it.

"Sure, I can do that for you. I like to play pool and drink a cold beer now and then. When do you want me to start?"

David looked at Todd, then back at Roger. "That's great! Anytime you can, the sooner the better, though. He brought in several boxes yesterday afternoon when we were riding yesterday. We almost met him on the road. We want to get all the facts before going to the police."

Roger's smile vanished. He didn't realize the boys were really serious and possibly in danger. This was not a game to be taken lightly.

"Okay, I'll go tonight. When you get out of school tomorrow come by and I'll let you know if I found out anything."

David looked at Todd, then back at Roger. "That would be great, Roger. Thanks. We really don't know how big this is, but it has my sister so curious we can't keep her out of the woods."

"I'll be careful."

Roger watched them climb back on the moped. With a final wave, they rode away. Thoughtfully Roger walked back to the car he was working on. He knew about the trouble the police were having with drugs being so freely available lately.

David must have stumbled onto the operation by accident and was now trying to put the pieces together. His friend Lenny would be at the pool hall and would probably know about the drugs.

Roger would have to be careful not to let slip about David's side of the story. Lenny was a friend to share drinks and a few stories, but not a close friend to be trusted with personal information.

It was after nine o'clock when Roger dressed in his black cowboy boots, favorite jeans and western shirt stepped up to the door of Scooters. As he opened the door, his nose was assaulted by the smell of stale tobacco smoke and whisky.

Smoke hovered around the light fixtures like fog. A juke box blared out an old country song by Hank Williams, Jr.. The clinking sound of pool balls hitting each other in the back room could be heard.

Even before he closed the door, Roger felt strange. The pool room seemed foreign to him. He had been away too long. Maybe that was it. Roger had started going to Church and had accepted Christ as his Savior.

Trying to stay straight was hard. He still loved to play pool, but not in this smoky atmosphere. He moved through the men standing around the bar and walked back toward the pool room. As he scanned the room with alert blue eyes, he noticed a couple of men dressed in suits he hadn't seen in town before.

They were sitting at a table drinking. No one locally was with them. Danger was there. The hairs on the back of his neck stood up. Should he stay? Nonchalantly he moved toward the pool tables on his left. The bar area was left behind along with the strangers.

Here was familiar territory. Another juke box was playing a different tune. Four tables were set up for play. One was being used right then. Roger looked at the players.

One was a local who did odd jobs at the hardware store. He always had money to spend. No one seemed curious to know where he got it. As the second man moved around the table chalking his stick, Roger recognized Ralph Snyder.

He could listen in, maybe by playing solo at the next table. He selected a cue stick from the rack. Putting a quarter in the slot, he released the balls from the shelf on the table. Setting the cue ball on the table, he began racking up the balls.

As he was chalking up his stick, he heard Ralph mention a boat. Grinning to himself, he broke his balls, starting his game. The more he listened, the more he enjoyed his game.

It was easier than he thought to 'spy' on someone. He moved around the table to get a better shot at the cue ball. This put him a little closer to the conversation without being suspicious to them.

Ralph mentioned the Old Mill and that Gary would be bringing in something really big the last Saturday of the month. Ralph's companion got excited and started talking party. Ralph inwardly grinned.

The clerk at the hardware store would spill the beans to the cops once he was caught. No threat there. He could almost enjoy questioning him at the hardware store without them knowing he was sort of on to them.

Ralph hushed him and told him to quiet down. They really shouldn't party yet. Ralph almost caught Roger staring at them while he was chalking up his stick. Swearing to himself, Roger resumed his game.

Before he decided to call it a night, he had heard plenty. Ralph had moved into the bar room to sit with the men with the suits. That part of the conversation Roger was not able to get in on.

Saturday would be another day to hang out there again. Something would take place there late next Saturday. Ralph mentioned a pickup and then a delivery there later that next Saturday.

Roger rammed the eight ball in his designated pocket, then stood up. He replaced the cue stick on the rack and strolled out of the bar. A cool fresh night air greeted him outside. Gratefully he breathed in the welcomed air. He then remembered why he had stopped attending the bars.

He didn't like the smell of whisky and stale tobacco on his clothes. It would take him a couple of days to get rid if the smell.

As he got into his pickup, he noticed Ralph now outside talking to the two strangers. One of them handed Ralph a thick envelope. Roger watched Ralph hand the men a small fat duffle bag.

Quickly Roger slid down on the truck seat to stay hidden while the men started their car and drove past him on their way out of town.

As the tailgate lights dimmed in the distance, Roger sat back up. The jeep with Ralph was heading the opposite direction. He started the truck and drove toward home. If David and Todd along with their sisters were involved, they were playing with dynamite. He would have to warn them off.

Roger saw them coming even from where he was under the car he was working on. All day he had tried to think of something to tell them. Slowly he pushed himself out and got to his feet. Wiping his hands off on his already stained jeans, he waited. Bright faces of expectation looked up at him. He had to go ahead and tell them what they wanted to know. Making a tug on his old cap, he stalked off toward the picnic table. Both boys followed him and sat down on the table top. Roger started pacing back and forth.

"Roger!"

Roger stopped and walked back to them. "All right. You guys are really in deep danger. This mystery is not a kids game like the Hardy Boys." He stopped and watched the boy's eyes grow larger with apprehension. Davie looked at Todd, then back at Roger.

"Fellas," Roger continued. "There were

strangers at Scooters last night and….."

Roger told them everything. Both boys listened to all the graphic details. As Roger talked, David began to realize the grave danger Charlie was in by riding alone in the woods. Somehow he either had to go with her or tell her flat out not to go near the Mill or the river. Roger sighed, heavily lifting his shoulders.

"That's the whole story. I can go back and see what is going down on Saturday, but….." He looked at the boys for an assent, but received none. "Well?"

David placed a hand on Todd's shoulder as he slid off the table. "We'll get back with you. We need to think this all out. We really appreciate your help and honesty, Roger. Can you at least pray about it? This seems like a big mystery."

Roger's neck turned red with embarrassment. Ducking his head, he mumbled a thanks. He had never received a thank you for anything this big. No one had ever appreciated his help before, let alone telling him so. When he looked up, the boys were gone. With another audible sigh, Roger walked back to his work.

Both boys went home. Todd followed David to his house. Charlie was busy in the barn cleaning the stalls. They heard her radio blaring as they opened the barn door. Surely the horses would be objecting the loud music.

All the stalls were empty. Charlie didn't see David and Todd enter the barn. Her head was swinging from side to side with the beat of the music. The *Newsboys* were singing their latest hit. The volume was almost full blast. Her pony tail was slowly falling down. Tuffs of hair was down around her ears as was some hanging down across her forehead.

She paid it no mind as she dug another shovelful of manure from the floor lifting it into the wheelbarrow. Out of the corner of her eye she caught a movement. Turning, she saw David and Todd. Lifting a hand in greeting, she leaned the shovel against the wall. David reached for the radio and turned it off.

"Where are the horses?" asked David.

"They took the day off. I put them in the back lot. Want to give me a hand?"

Instantly both boys clapped their hands.

"Ha ha, we have comedians in the crowd today. Do you have any funny stories to tell?"

"No, just a serious one. Take a break and come sit down. We need to talk."

Charlie looked from one to the other, her eyes then swiveling to stare at David. Silently she followed them over to a couple of bales of hay. Like Roger was when he told them the story of events, David paced some, then turned and told Charlie. She listened as he told her, looking for untruths or maybe skipping over important scary details. David had always been on the level with her and he was now.

She didn't want to stay out of the woods. She wanted to solve the mystery and help catch the bad guys. The strangers in town sounded like 'the mob'. Inwardly she shivered. The stories she had heard and read were not something she should take lightly. Nervously she plucked a couple hay stems from the bale; twisting them around her fingers as she listened to David. As he finished, she looked up into David's eyes, seeing the concerned look.

"What do you think we ought to do?"

"We can't do anything, really. We only know about the two men in the woods. We haven't any proof or evidence to give to the authorities."

"How can we get more evidence if we can't go in the woods? Roger told you it's too dangerous. Chief Walker won't pay attention to our story. We need to go back to the Mill and find something to show the Chief."

"Well, I guess we can do that. But you can't go alone, Charlie. What do you say, Todd? Do you want to ride with us?"

"Sure. Roger said Saturday will be the big day. We can get an early start that morning. Right now, I'd better get home and do my homework or Mom won't let me go anywhere."

Todd got up and said his goodbyes. David turned to Charlie.

"Let me help you here." He easily took hold of the wheelbarrow's handlebars and pushed it over to the next stall. Charlie handed him the extra shovel and began where she had left off. Her mind was twirling with thoughts about the Mill and the two men.

"David, do you really think we can do this? We have seen movies on TV where the bad guys really hurt the good guys. They….."

"Easy, Charlie. We'll be careful. They know we ride in the woods, but not where we live or who we are. We haven't told the authorities so they should feel safe so far. Saturday we will look around for evidence and take it to the Chief. From then on out, we'll let the authorities take over."

"Okay, but will we be all going into the woods again? Together?"

"Yes, but a different route. We'll take the one we found that comes out at the Blockhouse. That is halfway between the Mill and the river. We should be able to watch them from there. Let's get the horses back into the barn so we can get them fed and us cleaned up before Dad comes home. I think I am in charge of the evening devotions tonight. Will you say the prayer?"

Charlie nodded. Prayer. That was the

answer! They needed to pray about this situation and have God help them be safe.

Together they walked outside and started walking through the back pasture to round up the horses.

Chapter Five

"Hey! It's one of those kids! Get them!" boomed Ralph. Heavy footfalls crunched across the dry palmetto leaves. Someone grabbed a rifle. "No killing. Just shoot to scare."

Charlie's heart was in her mouth as she ran through the brush. Her hands fanned out in front of her to push back the branches from her path. She had gone too far this time. She stumbled over a tree root, caught herself and ran again. Her shirt caught on a bush, resisting, then tearing. Charlie's mouth was dry. Seeing Peanut where she had left him tied gave her a small sense of relief. She still had to get away.

Jerking the reins loose from the bush, she swung onto Peanut's back in one fluid motion. Grabbing a handful of mane, she bent low over his neck, digging into its sides. Sensing the urgency of the situation, Peanut laid his ears back and stretched out in a full run. Behind her came the yells of the three men. A gun fired sending a loud report echoing through the trees. Birds flew from their nightly perches screeching in protest. Charlie didn't even know what trail she was running on as long as it was heading away from the danger. At the sound of the jeep in pursuit, Charlie checked Peanut's speed. She could not outrun a jeep for very long. She was a long way from the edge of the forest. In an opening just wide enough for Peanut to clear, Charlie turned into the brush.

Carefully she wound around through the trees. Thankfully there was enough daylight left to see her way around. A narrow trail was crossed as she stuck to the undergrowth where no tracks could be seen.

A long fifteen minutes passed before she rode into a small clearing. There sat the Old mill! Somehow she had gotten turned around. Muttering a few bad words, she wheeled Peanut around toward a trail she definitely knew would lead towards home. Peanut trotted along as Charlie kept an eye peeled for the men and the jeep.

Just as she thought she was safe, Peanut spooked. A deer leaped across the road. Peanut half-reared, twirled around, then charged down an unfamiliar trail. "Peanut! Whoa!" Charlie clung to Peanut's back for dear life. He was running away! She had been warned about this but she had never took it seriously or paid attention to things you could do to stop a runaway.

Grinding wheels of the jeep in the gravel road sounded too close for comfort. Suddenly the bright glare of the jeep's headlights pierced the darkness around Charlie. Frightened beyond screaming, Charlie was able to whirl Peanut onto a trail leading to the right. Swiftly Peanut ran toward home. The jeep stopped its pursuit. The kid was scared good now and would not be returning. Ralph chuckled as he stepped out of the jeep and fired the rifle toward the departing rider. Charlie turned slightly around at the rifle firing. As she turned back something solid hit her head knocking her off Peanut and unconscious. She hit the ground hard and skidded several feet before she stopped and laid still. Peanut had been trained to stay with its rider if they ever parted company.

With all the scary things that had just taken place, it forgot all of its training and ran for home and the safety of its barn stall.

Night claimed the forest as the sun disappeared in the West. All was quiet except crickets and tree frogs. A lone osprey screeched in the distance. Slowly Charlie opened her eyes and brushed away whatever was tickling her face. As she moved her head, she felt the blinding pain causing her to gasp. Her hands gingerly felt her head. There was no blood. Hadn't she been shot? She had heard the rifle…. Oh,no she was still in the woods and it was dark! David would definitely kill her this time. Where was Peanut? Rolling over on her side she felt other parts that hurt. Her elbows were skinned and her knees felt like they were too under her jeans. Slowly Charlie sat up and stuck a hand in front of her face. It was so dark that she couldn't see her hand. There was no moon to guide her and she didn't know what direction was home. Peanut had left her. Should she start walking toward home? Everything was hurting now. Once more she tried to stand, but her head hurt so bad, she dropped back down to her hands and knees.

On hands and knees Charlie crawled out onto the trail. Using her hands, she felt for Peanut's hoof print. Her hands located one, but it was an old one and she couldn't depend on that one to guide her the right direction. Slowly she tried to stand up. Dizziness forced her to sit down again. Her head was pounding with pain. Tears welled up in her eyes. Several tears slipped down her dirty dusty cheeks. What was she going to do now? Even if Peanut did find his way home, no one would come looking for her until morning. No voices or sounds of the jeep could be heard.

They had left her thinking she was long gone and was never coming back into the woods again. They had no way of knowing she had fallen off her pony and was still there nearby. The scare they had given her was all they felt was necessary to keep her from them and the Mill. They did not know Charlie and her vast curiosity in the mystery that was there in 'her' woods. If she was lucky she might be able to sit down after her parents got through with her.

Angrily as well as frustrated, Charlie hit the ground with a doubled fist.

Slowly she tried getting to her feet once

more. On wobbly legs, she slowly walked in the rut of a trail. Every so often she would get down and search for hoof prints. All of the trails eventually led to the main one leading out and home. All she had to worry about was crossing it and going off in another different direction.

It was close to midnight when Charlie located what she thought was the main trail. Ramming her hand in her jeans pocket, she pulled out a single match. Crossing her fingers, she struck it. It flickered and stayed lit as she grabbed some Spanish moss from a branch to use for fuel. It caught fire. Carefully Charlie wrapped some around a heavy stick and used it for a torch to show her the trail. It didn't put out much light, but enough to see the trail and the recent tracks from Peanut's shoes. It was slow going as she walked with her head pounding and having to stop to stamp out the falling ashes from the burning stick and moss. Rustling sounds in the bushes kept her on the move. It could only be a possum or a raccoon, but she wasn't about to wait around and find out.

An owl hooted nearby. The cool night air caused the trees to rustle as the branches rubbed against each other. Charlie shivered with cold. A sob caught in her throat. She wanted to be home in bed. How much farther was the main trail going before she would be safely on the road toward home. Silently she prayed for a rescue.

The droning sound of a motor caused her to

jerk her head up. A single headlight probed through the darkness bouncing along the road. Her name was yelled out from the darkness. "Charlie!"

David! He was on his moped. He had come looking for her! Standing to her feet, she waved the burning stick. "Over here, David!" her voice was just above a croak, but he heard her. Oh, did she ever hurt!

Slowly, too slowly the headlight came toward her. As the headlight reached her, she stepped into its light.

"Charlie!" David rammed down the foot stand, leaving the bike on idle. Swinging his long legs over he stepped toward Charlie to wrap an arm around his shivering sister.

"What happened?"

"It's a long story. Peanut ran under a branch and I hit my head. I forgot to duck."

"He's supposed to stay with you." David took off his jacket and helped her put it on. He couldn't see the large welt on her forehead where the knot stood out. He turned the bike around and got back on the seat.

Charlie climbed on behind him, wrapping her arms around his waist. Closing her eyes to the jarring pain she withstood the rough jolting ride back to the main trail and home!

As they neared the yard, David cut the motor and climbed off. Charlie slid up into the driver's seat as David pushed the bike into the yard and to the barn where he kept it.

Charlie climbed off. David caught her as she stumbled against him.

"Hey, you're really hurt! Poor kid!" Gently David guided Charlie to a chair near the sink in the barn. Finding a clean cloth, he ran warm water over it. As he wrung out the excess water, he spoke again. "I suppose we need to keep this from our parents, too.

What did you see back there?"

Charlie winced as he laid the damp cloth against an open cut near the knot.

"There were three guys at the Old Mill. One of them was Ralph who drives the jeep. He picked up the other two from the dock. I guess he comes from somewhere along the river. They were talking about coke and uppers and downers some guys at the bar wanted. I didn't realize I was crouching almost in the open. It was dark and when they happened to turn on the jeep headlights to see something, they saw me. I flew out of there and got off the trail. They were……" she hesitated. Should she tell him they were actually shooting a gun at her? David swabbed another cut, stopping as she stopped speaking.

"They were…… Come on, Charlie. Tell me

the whole story. We're in this together, remember?"

Charlie nodded, holding a hand behind her back with her fingers crossed. "I think they were shooting a gun at me. That's why Peanut didn't stay with me when I got knocked off. She's never been shot at before."

David put the cloth down and found some peroxide. His sister was a spunky kid, but living dangerously now. Those men saw her and could probably recognize her on the streets downtown. So far he had been unsuccessful in keeping Charlie out of harms way. She simply refused to keep out of the woods now that danger abounded. He almost wished they had not discovered the Old Mill. Somehow he would have to take time to try to solve the mystery and make the woods safe again. Right now, though, he needed to get Charlie up to her room.

"When you get upstairs, take a couple of aspirins. That will probably help your headache. Luckily there is no school tomorrow so you can sleep late. Can you stand up?"

Slowly Charlie stood up. She really needed a hot bath, but that would be impossible. Their parents would hear the water running and it was really late. She wondered how David covered her absence.

" How did you get Peanut back in her stall without mom and dad knowing?"

"I couldn't sleep and was on the front porch. I heard Peanut running, so I figured you must have fallen off somewhere you were not supposed to be. Mom and Dad had already retired to their room to watch TV.

Good thing I sort of knew where you were. I got the Moped and pushed it quite a ways before I started her up. I'm glad I had gas in it. Charlie, you have to stay out of the woods. With a little questioning around town, they can easily figure out who you are and where we live. Time is very important now if we plan to catch them and turn them over to the authorities. Right now, we need to get you in the house."

She definitely had a great brother. She also knew that to keep him that way, she needed to go easy. He really sounded concerned for her safety and had risked a lot sneaking out after their parents had gone to bed. He could have told them and created a huge scene. Charlie set her chin with a silent resolve to try to be more responsible.

Getting up to her room was easy as some other house noises muffled the squeak in one of the steps going upstairs. David followed her into her room and helped her take off her shoes and socks. Taking a shower was out until morning. He retrieved the aspirins and a glass of water for her while she got into her pj's. Slowly she crawled under the covers and fell back onto her pillow. Man! Was she ever tired!   As the aspirins began to work, sleep came easily for Charlie. David watched her fall asleep from her doorway. A frown on his forehead as he worried his lip across his teeth. Expelling a sigh, he turned and went back to his room. All was quiet now in the house. Their parent's TV had been turned off. What to do? How could he keep her home without the parents getting suspicious about not letting her go riding?

<h1 style="text-align:center">Chapter Six</h1>

The following weekend the four friends decided to go riding together. Charlie's head had healed up and she was able to cover the knot with a change in hairdo. It was a subdued Charlie the rest of that week, much to the approval of David. Their lives were in danger and caution had to be number one.

Cautiously the riders circled the small clearing. Ahead of them stood the grey walls of the Old Mill ruins. Before it had been a historical find; now it was danger.

That Saturday morning was an important trip for the riders. They were to search the Mill and the river front for evidence of drug smuggling. As far as the group knew, the men meeting in the woods were busy in town. David had called Roger and he confirmed that Ralph and his buddies were busy in their store. They therefore felt safe to venture about around the Old Mill and the river road.

Lisa was leading the group as everyone relaxed and letting their horses nibble grass as they pleased. Todd had just let the reins slide through his hand as his gelding bit off some tall grass. A loud sound like an Indian war whoop shattered their silence. Todd's horse's head snapped up as it whirled around. Both boys were grapping their saddle horns to stay on as they tried to pull up the loose reins.

Lisa was just barely in the saddle as her horse almost sat down before whirling around. Her horse pivoted around practically on top of the other horses. The Indian had jumped right in front of her! Where had it come from? His ugly red and black painted head reared back shaking a long barreled rifle in the air at her. Bushes rustled off to the side and parts of another Indian figure part way emerged. Instantly Charlie knew they were *really* in danger now. She was also scrambling to stay aboard Peanut.

David and Todd were swinging their horses around to get away, too. Charlie glanced back and saw the Indian raise a long barreled rifle before Peanut broke into a run for the open road.

She glanced back again seeing the Indian take aim with the rifle. She flattened down across Peanut's neck as the loud crack of the muzzle loader fired. All four horses were at a dead run down the narrow trail.

Tree branches and thorny vines lashed out at the horses and riders, tearing clothes and scratching their arms. Once they were back near the main trail towards home, did the horses calm down enough for their riders to gain full control.

David finally got his grey mare to slow down and stopped her. The other horses slid to a halt rather than run into David's mare. Everyone was breathing hard. The grey rolled her eyes and let out a loud snort. Charlie reined Peanut up beside the others.

"Did you see it?"

"Not very well. Who fired at us?" replied Todd.

Only the girls had actually seen the Indians because they had been leading. Both Indians had vanished into the bushes after firing the one shot. Both boys had all they could handle handling their horses and staying on them. They hadn't been looking for what had caused their scare.

"It was an Indian with a long barreled rifle. He shot at us. We'd better get out of here!"

The grey tossed her head jerking on the reins. On her own, she turned down the narrow trail once more with the others following. If anyone could find their way home from being in a strange place, she could. Slowly they single filed after the mare. All were in a hurry to get home, their goal to search the mill forgotten.

Their horses were wet with sweat from a long run to escape the sudden appearance of an Indian on the trail. Neither of them believed in ghosts, but whatever had jumped out onto the trail was not supposed to be there.

The four rode down farther to another section where more open trails were located. It was across from their favorite riding woods and this one was used by ATV riders and hikers. Along the side of the trail was an old picnic table where they stopped to examine their scratches and torn clothing.

Todd took off his bandana and rubbed the sweat off his face. He had never been so scared in all his life! Stealing a glance over at the others, he noted they were sweating and acted scared too. Truly playing computer games was a lot safer! He noticed that Charlie's pony, Peanut, wanted to go home.

It kept pulling on the bridle forcing her to hang on tightly. His sister was shaken, too. She had been leading the group. Her pony, also, was trying to head back toward home.

"Our horses want to go home, but it is really too early to call the end of our ride for this weekend. Do you think the horses will let us go on this trail and then turn around toward home?"

David shrugged his shoulders. His mare was standing quietly, probably because she felt safe now. He patted her neck and turned toward Charlie who was still trying to calm Peanut down. Two huge scares within a week had made the pony really jumpy.

"What do you think, Charlie? Do we want to ride further?"

"This 'tame' trail does have some nice side roads narrower than a ATV can handle. Sure. Let's go!"

All excited to continue their weekend ride, the riders checked their saddles and remounted. Charlie moved Peanut up in front so she could show them the side trails. The ride would not be as adventurous but the excitement was over for the day.

Back at the mill site.   "How'd I do, Ralph?" replied the Indian. He walked up to the jeep and laid the rifle across the hood. He pulled off the headdress.

"Great! I never saw such a ruckus. Those kids won't be back in here for several days, at least. Let's go check the Mill and make sure they didn't go back in there."

The man grabbed the rifle and put it in the back of the jeep, then swung a long leg into the jeep.

Ralph started the engine while the man got settled in the seat. Ralph shifted gears and started down the deep rutted trail leading to the Mill.

"Can I get a fix now, Ralph?" The man said as he grabbed a rag to wash off the war paint.

"Just wait a little longer. We need to make sure the coast is clear."

"Do you think we will need to do this again?"

"No." laughed Ralph. "I don't think so. If

the kids didn't scare, their horses did and they won't want to return anytime soon."

The man dipped the rag into some water and began washing off the make-up from his face. That had been fun. He had never fired a muzzle loader before or seen what it would do to scare horses. Inwardly he grinned. All in a day's work for a fix that would make him feel good for several hours.

Ralph dropped the man off in town at his home. He then returned to the lawnmower shop. He still had a couple of parts to order for a customer and put some parts on a mower waiting to be picked up. Summer was coming and the business would soon be picking up. People needed their lawnmowers working properly.

All the way back to the Thomas's, Todd and Lisa could not wait to get on home. The horses continued acting up and pulling on the reins to run. All of them had to hold on tight to keep them at a slow trot and walk.

No one talked along the rough return home. They had tried to ride at a leisurely pace along the new trails Charlie showed them, but they ended up fighting the horses who wanted to go home in the worst way.

In the yard, Todd and Lisa waved farewell and headed on down the driveway to go home. They didn't stop for refreshments that Mrs.

Thomas had prepared. She looked out the kitchen window and watched them ride off. That was unusual for the boys. She knew that David had another new game he was dying for Todd to see. Wiping her hands on the dishcloth, she busied herself with early dinner preparations.

They had had enough excitement for one day. It was not even lunchtime either. Charlie watched them go as they dismounted and began unsaddling the horses. They turned them loose in the corral so they could roll and calm down. Charlie put her gear on the rack in the tack room. David plopped his saddle down on his rack.

"What do you think?"

"Charlie, I think someone is trying to scare us and to keep us out of the woods and away from the Mill. Maybe we'd better lay low for a week. According to Roger's information, we have over a week before their big day."

"Yeah, but what if Mom and Dad want to go riding tomorrow? We can't have an Indian jumping in front of them."

"We'll stick to the trails up at this end and near the lakes. We can ride all the way to the river along the road to the State Park. Dad's been curious about how far we could go on that land near the road. We can find out then. Let's get our chores done."

Several days passed before David saw his

chance to ride back into the woods. Charlie had gone to town with their Mom. David put his zoom lens on his camera and packed it carefully in the saddlebags.

As he rode past the old dead tree, a young Osprey landed on one of the top branches. When David looked up to see the bird, he felt a tug on the reins. Liz had lowered her head for a clump of grass. He let her get a bite, then pulled her head up to go on. He was anxious to get going. Overlooking the twin lakes, he took a deep breath.

So beautiful! A sudden movement above his head made him look up.

The young Osprey took off in flight and headed for the lakes. Gracefully it circled above the water before swooping down to snag an unsuspecting fish in its talons. With a cry of success, it rose up into the sky once more and returned to the tree branch with the fish securely in its claws.

David shook his head slowly in awe. Nature's happenings always intrigued him. How anyone could deny the presence of God, he didn't know.

He took a few seconds to focus his camera on the Osprey and snapped a couple of pictures. Replacing the camera in its bag, he once more gathered the reins to continue across the lakes and into the woods.

It was so relaxing to sit in the shade of the large Oak tree there on the hill and look out across the lakes to the woods beyond. Who would believe that evil now ran free behind the lakes?

Just as David started between the lakes, he spotted the jeep coming from the other way entering the same trail he was about to take. Liz tossed her head as she tried to get more slack in the reins. One large juicy clump of grass was just outside her reach. Her lips popped as she tried to grab the grass in her teeth.

David allowed her the extra rein to grab the grass. He was now in no hurry to get on the same trail as Ralph in the jeep. Hopefully Ralph was not looking around and would see him standing there.

Liz contently chewed the grass while her eyes searched for more. David nudged her with his heels. With a little grunt of protest, Liz raised her head and started walking once more.

Keeping a safe distance and off the trail from the fast moving jeep was easier than David thought. He used his ears to listen for the motor and shifting of gears instead of visual. He didn't want to risk being seen.

After determining the jeep was headed for the Mill, rather than the river, David reined Liz off onto their smaller trail. Quickly he moved her down the trail to the backside of the Mill.

Slowly he moved between the palmetto fronds trying not to make too much noise.

As he came closer, he looked carefully around and listened for the jeep in case Ralph changed his mind about his direction. He heard the grinding of the jeep's gears as Ralph slowed down enough to make the turn onto the trail leading to the Mill.

David dismounted, tying Liz to a tree. He pulled out the camera from his saddlebags and made minor adjustments, then found a good spot to watch the driver.

Ralph climbed out of the jeep and went to the back to drop its tailgate down. He then went to the hidden well and crouched down beside his hiding place. Scraping away the leaves covering the weathered board, he lifted it up.

Sliding it over, he reached down grabbing the large sack. Sitting it down beside him, he reached back for a second one. With the board back in place, he swept the leaves over the board making sure it was well covered before he stood up.

Satisfied that it looked natural with the surrounding area he picked up the bags. He carried them over to the jeep and tossed them into the back, then slammed the tailgate up in place. He was unaware of David hidden in the palmettos snapping pictures of him.

David focused the zoom lens then shot in

rapid succession. He sighed in relief as Ralph drove away. He sure hoped the shots came out.

He didn't need to know what was in the bags right now. He needed to get back home. He replaced the camera in his saddlebags, then untied Liz and mounted.

He took a different small trail that was somewhat a short cut that would take him home without the danger of running into Ralph in the jeep. He allowed himself a smile of satisfaction and let Liz have her head. Liz shook her head, then fast walked toward home and her feed bin.

Charlie was holding an armload of packages by their car trunk in the grocery store parking lot when Ralph drove past. She ducked behind their car to keep out of sight. She really didn't know if Ralph would recognize her or did he even notice her in the parking lot?

She watched the jeep drive on down the street and stop in front of the bar. Charlie frowned. She wondered what he was doing so she watched him get out of the jeep and go to the back, pulling out several sacks.

Wow! In broad daylight! What was he up to? Charlie rubbed her itching nose on her shirt sleeve. Something was up. She could hardly wait to tell David when she got home.

When they came in the yard, Charlie saw David out by the fence line. He had posthole diggers and a small roll of wire. She watched him jab the digger into the ground.

Smiling, she instantly was thankful she was a girl. Gratefully she took a bag of groceries from the car trunk. She might be a tomboy, but she knew the feminine way of life.

Leaving her mom to prepare the evening meal, Charlie went upstairs to shower and change clothes. David found her hopping on one foot to put on a tennis shoe. She finally shoved her foot into the already laced up shoe and saw David standing in her doorway.

"I saw the man in the jeep in town awhile ago." she told him.

"I did too." replied David and began telling her about his trip in the woods.

Chapter Seven

Roger looked at the pictures David had taken of Ralph. Together they made tentative plans to catch him in the act of receiving the drugs. Roger borrowed a friend's boat and would be on the river to watch for Gary's boat to dock near the Mill.

Chief Watkins was notified after being shown the pictures David had taken. He would follow Ralph with a couple of deputies. Everything was falling in place.

Todd and Lisa wanted to be there, too. Charlie could hardly contain herself. Several times she almost got her parents suspecting them in some type of mischief. With them off on a golf game for the day, the four horse people headed for the woods.

Even the horses sensed the kid's excitement. It was Saturday and the day Ralph and his buddies had been waiting for. They were not even suspicious of what was transpiring with the law and the four horse riders.

Gary had met with their contact people just outside the waterway heading into the State Park. Under the bridge they had exchanged money and the drugs. No one knew of their location so no one was watching. As Gary left the two men in their speed boat, he slowly made his way toward the broken down dock where Ralph would be waiting.

He could hardly control his excitement. Now, he could be fixed for life with the amount of drugs that were in his care. Ralph would also split the money with him when they sold their drugs to the people waiting in town. Things were really looking up.

There had been no more signs of the kids and their horses. Gary laughed. His Indian get-up must have really done the trick. He took the bend in the river and zeroed into the dock. Ralph was not there. This was the mother lode. He would have to get out of the boat and help load the jeep once the boat was emptied. Gary cut the motor and coasted up to the bank. He hopped out and scrambled up the slippery bank. Tying off the boat, he stood there looking back down the trail. Where was he? Was he early? Gary glanced down at his wrist, then remembered his watch had stopped working the day before and he had never replaced it. He reached in his pocket and pulled out a cigarette, then lit it. Smoking sometimes calmed his nerves and they were really jumpy. This was an important load. Right now it was safe inside the boat.

Carefully David led Charlie, Todd and Lisa around behind the Mill. In the distance they could hear a motor but wasn't sure if it was the jeep. The river was a ten minute ride from the

Mill by horseback.

"Todd, you are in charge here. Keep out of sight and be on the lookout for the sheriff and his men. They are following Ralph in the jeep. Roger is with a deputy in a boat watching for the boat Ralph is waiting on to come. You stay near by and keep Charlie and Lisa safe. I'm going on toward the river and see how things are going."

David left the three there at the Mill. By going around another way, he could ride a parallel trail to the river. He needed to check on the boat. Roger and one of the deputies in their boat should be somewhere nearby.

Roger and the sheriff's deputy slowly maneuvered their boat around in the canal out of sight from Gary in his boat. From where they sat, Gary would not be able to leave the broken down dock where he was now tied up. The deputy had radioed ahead to another sheriff's car about the boat under the bridge that needed following. Soon, everyone would be caught and hopefully everyone would be safe from danger.

The sheriff and other men should be along behind Ralph and his men soon.

Hopefully Charlie could stay hidden along with Todd and Lisa.

Grinding gears of the jeep were soon heard. Charlie couldn't see anyone following. Maybe they were further back. Hopefully they were just back there keeping out of sight. Turning her attention back to Ralph she saw that he had someone with him. The three watched them digging up some bags from a hole. Ralph was cleaning out the stash to take to town and sell. The boxes on the soon to arrive boat, would be back-up. Ralph slowly grinned to himself. This was really big! He could almost see the new electronic gadgets he was going to purchase with his share of the take.

Charlie tapped Todd on the shoulder. Whispering, she said. "I wonder if we should distract them so the sheriff can get here?"

Todd shook his head. "I'll go back to the main trail and see if I can find the sheriff. Stay put, both of you." The girls watched him go behind them and start through the palmettos.

All was quiet except for the men digging in the hole, pulling out bags and taking them to the jeep. Charlie gritted her teeth. She hated waiting! It would be a good half hour before David could get back to them. Charlie glanced around her. Lisa was gone! Where was she?

Lisa got a cramp in her leg and had moved away from where Charlie was. She hadn't meant to move so far away, but the coast looked clear. She had seen one of the men walk off . Hoping that he hadn't seen her, she stood back up to stretch the cramping calf muscle. Suddenly a big arm flashed out and around her neck jerking her back against him. She opened her mouth to scream, a large dirty hand covered her mouth.

Lisa could smell whiskey along with tobacco scent on it. She forced herself not to gag.

"Don't even think about yelling, kid." he hissed in her ear. His hot liquored smelling breath assaulted her nostrils. Roughly he jerked her alongside him toward the others by the hole. "Hey, Ralph, look what I found."

Ralph recognized Lisa. She had been in his lawn mower repair shop with her dad several times. Joe had a tight hold on her. Lisa was scared. She tried to stay calm, but she was shaking anyhow. This was no time to fall apart. Somewhere out there was help. They could not harm her. They didn't need kidnapping or child abuse attached to what they were doing now against the law.

"Tie and gag her. The others are probably out there spying on us. She wouldn't have come alone. Gary should be at the dock about now. We need to get loaded and out of here pronto!"

"What about the kid?"

"Put her down in the well. The spiders can keep her company."

Taking a hold of Lisa's bound hands, they lifted her up and down into the well. Cobwebs clung to her as she wiggled about before they let go. She landed on her feet and stood in the middle trying not to think of the spiders. She rubbed her face against her sleeve to free the remains of a cobweb stuck there. Lisa heard the jeep rev up its motor and drive away. She knew Charlie was nearby, so she didn't have to panic.

Nearby the police and Todd watched the jeep drive off toward the river. They stopped Ralph at the main trail with their guns pointed. Ralph and Joe were taken out of the jeep and handcuffed, then placed in the back of their squad car.

No one had seen Lisa being captured and put in the well. Todd was told to go get the girls and their horses, then ride back toward home.

Charlie almost screamed when Todd came up beside her. He told her what the chief wanted. Charlie told Todd what had happened to Lisa. Together they moved toward the well. Looking down at Lisa, she was too far down to reach.

"Lisa, we can't reach you. Will you be all right until we get back with help?"

Lisa muffled a noise. They got on their horses and rode out to the main trail.

Leaving Lisa's horse there, they quickly found a couple of the policemen. A police van was down the road a ways and was loading the men in the jeep into it.

One of the officers was putting on Ralph's ball cap and climbing into the jeep. They were preparing to drive to the river and pick up Gary and the shipment. Charlie and Todd rode up beside the jeep.

"Charlie, how about riding in the jeep with Peter and show him where the river dock is."

Charlie eagerly slid off Peanut and climbed into the jeep. "Lisa is down in the well back at the Mill. She's tied up and we couldn't get her out."

"We'll get her."

A couple of the other officers climbed into the back of the jeep and off they went to the river.

David knelt behind a large palmetto tree watching Gary standing there smoking a second cigarette. David heard the jeep coming and went further back in the underbrush to watch.

As the jeep came closer, Gary saw the kid in the seat beside Ralph. What was she doing in there? Had Ralph lost his mind? What were they going to do with a kid? All caution was dropped as he angrily stomped off to meet the jeep. Gary hadn't even suspected a trap. In an instant everything would be all over.

"Howdy, Pardoe. Hands up!" called one of the officers from the back of the jeep as he swung his legs over the tailgate and hurried around as he pulled out his gun.

Shocked by the sudden appearance of the lawmen, Gary spun around to run back toward the dock and his boat. David leaped out between him and the riverbank. Scrambling in the mud along the bank, Gary tried to break free from David's grasp on his collar.

"Leggo, Kid! I gotta get out of here!" Frantically he struggled free of David's grasp. David grabbed him again and they rolled down the slippery riverbank into the water beside the boat. Gary swung at David, hitting his chin and breaking David's hold on him. He would have gotten away, but not before two other hands were on him forcing him to the ground. His hands were pulled behind him and handcuffs were snapped in place. The officer pulled him to his feet and took him over to the jeep. David sloshed back upon the bank. Mud dripped in thick rivets down his wet clothes and hair. Charlie ran up to him.

"David! Are you okay?"

"Sure. Did you get caught?"

"No. Lisa did. They put her in the abandoned well with spiders. I came along for the ride to show them how to find the dock. I'm sure glad it wasn't me in there! It had to be crawling with spiders and all kinds of creepy crawly things. Did we get everything?"

"Uh, Charlie, Liz probably won't like for me to be on her with all this mud and water. Can you ride her back home? I don't think I could stay on with this slippery mud, either. I'll hitch a ride in the jeep. They can drop me off at home."

"Okay. Where is she?"

Charlie found Liz contently eating a circle around the tree where she was tied. Liz pricked up her ears at the sight of Charlie, then looked beyond her for David.

Softly she nickered.

"Sorry, girl, but you will have to put up with me. Now, hold still."

Once in the saddle, she gathered up the reins and hung on tight. She was on a big powerful horse that would probably try to head for home faster than Charlie could handle her to go. She would also take off if she knew she was alone in the woods.

"Hel…….loo." called someone.

"Lisa! Over here!"

Lisa came riding up and turned her horse beside Liz and Charlie. Her face broke into a wide grin. "Well, we did it! We solved the mystery of the Old Mill and caught the bad guys. No more danger for us in the woods. The chief wants us to come to town tomorrow and tell our story after school. Are you going to tell your mom and dad?"

Charlie groaned out loud. She could just visualize the punishment she would receive once her parents realized what she had been doing every time she went riding. "I'll have to. Our names will be all over the paper. We'll be heroes. Hummmm. I wonder if there is another mystery somewhere that we can solve?"

"Oh, Charlie!"

Addison Blockhouse Historic State Park

The State Library and Archives of Florida hold a map of the John Addison plantation from 1816. Addison first acquired the land in 1807 and named the plantation, "Carrickfergus" after his birthplace in Ireland. The 1816 map shows that the plantation covered 1,414 acres from the west bank of the Tomoka River to the Kings Road. Addison grew cotton and other field crops in the area shown as "cleared land" on the 1816 map. The labor for clearing, planting, picking, and ginning cotton was provided by 63 enslaved workers. John Addison died in 1825 and was buried on his plantation by his brother, Thomas Addison. The plantation was sold two years later to Duncan and Kenneth McCrae. The McCraes built a large steam-powered sugar mill in 1832 that operated for four years.

In 1836, Seminole warriors King Philip and Wildcat led a raid on Carrickfergus, destroying the sugar mill and other plantation buildings. After the Seminole raids, the plantation was abandoned and the Addison gravesite disappeared until 1911 when the Daytona Gazette-News reported that an unknown grave had been found in the woods along the Tomoka River. The identity of the grave was later revealed when the broken headstone was found nearby in the woods with the inscription, "Sacred to the Memory of John Addison." The headstone was repaired and placed at the Recreation Hall at Tomoka State Park where it is now protected from vandalism and natural decay. Today all that stands is what is believed to be the outdoor kitchen of the Addison plantation and partial walls and foundations of the McCrae sugar mill.

There is little access to Addison Blockhouse Historic State Park aside from the Tomoka River. At times there are lead interpretative hikes or historical society outings to visit the ruins. Pleas contact Tomoka State Park at 386-676-4075 with any questions about Addison Blockhouse Historic State Park

About the Author

Laura E. Federmeyer grew up in a small town in Ohio where she lived with her parents and two younger sisters. She had always liked to make up stories and write bout horses and cowboys. As a teenager, she accepted Christ and began writing stories for church publications. A couple of her works were printed and she won second place in a writing contest.

She moved to Florida in 1967. She met an older lady who had horses and cattle and Laura was able to fulfill one of her dreams of being a cowboy. Several years later she was able to own her own horse.

Her next dream was having a home in the country and that came true when she married her husband Richard. Now, both are retired, enjoying country life and serving their small church. This is Laura's second book. Her first was published December 2013 – Loren's Journey of Faith.